N is for NORTH KOREA

Written by **Trevor Eissler**
Illustrated by **Matthew J. Baek**

*To my mom and her family who escaped
North Korea by rowboat, in the darkness.*
– MJB

Written by Trevor Eissler.
Illustrated by Matthew J. Baek.

Cataloging-in-Publication Data

Eissler, Trevor
N is for North Korea

Includes 30 illustrations
1. North Korea 2. South Korea 3. Korea—Fiction 4. Children's fiction
FIC E Eis P27.P173 Ei 2012
ISBN: 978-0-9822833-2-5

S EVENOFF

www.Sevenoff.com

Printed in U.S.A.

Na-young had two pet grasshoppers, one green and one brown.

During the day, when Na-young was at school, her grasshoppers lived in a square box. Na-young poked several tiny air holes in the lid of the box, too small for the grasshoppers to escape while she was away. The brown one loved to stay in the box, but the green one always tried to climb out. Na-young often played with them as soon as she got home from school.

One summer evening, after the sun finally set, Na-young put her grasshoppers back in the box. She said good night to her mother and father. She climbed into bed and pulled the sheets up tight. But she could not sleep.

Na-young tossed and turned. She pushed the blankets down. She pulled the blankets up. She turned on her left side, then turned on her right. She still could not sleep. She was not thinking about school, nor was she thinking about her favorite yellow dress. She was not even thinking about her grasshoppers. No, this was something she had never thought of before. She was thinking about a cousin. Her cousin! A girl she had never met. A girl just like herself.

Earlier that afternoon, Na-young's father had told her the exciting news that she had a cousin in South Korea. Imagine that! Father said her cousin was also eight years old! Na-young had no brothers or sisters, so the thought of having her own cousin made her happy. Maybe her cousin liked to play with grasshoppers, too?

She was so excited! But when she asked if she could call her cousin on the phone, her father said, "No."

"Can I write her a letter in an envelope?"

"No."

"Can I go visit her?"

"No." He shook his head and looked down. Na-young felt sad.

The next morning Na-young's father whispered in her ear that he was going to bring home a present for her from the Arirang Festival. After he left, Na-young couldn't sit still all day. She couldn't wait for her father to return home. She looked out the window. She sat on the doorstep. She kicked stones in the front walk. She stood on the stump. She walked out to the street and gazed up the road for a long time.

Finally, there he was!

Her father came over the hill riding
his bicycle carefully with one hand, the
other hand holding tightly to a bright
red helium-filled balloon!

She squealed with delight!

After her father brought the balloon inside, he let her hold it. Her mother and father reminded Na-young to hold the string tightly if the door was open, so the wind wouldn't blow the balloon away and up into the sky.

Na-young made sure the front door was closed. She pulled her hand down close to the floor and let the balloon go! It quickly rose up to the ceiling and stayed there. The long string hung down just far enough for Na-young to grab it again. She pulled it down and released it again. And again. Her mother and father laughed and smiled at each other. She tied the string to her finger and walked around the house. She tied the string to her hair. Her hair stuck straight up in the air!

She tied it to a pencil. The pencil flew!

Suddenly she had a wonderful idea. It was so wonderful that she had to sit down. She closed her eyes. She let the idea snuggle up and get cozy in her brain. What if she attached a note to the string and let the balloon float from her house in North Korea to her cousin in South Korea?

Na-young didn't tell her mother or father about her idea. She waited until the next day when she was all alone in the house. She found a pencil and a large piece of cardboard and wrote, "Hi. My name is Na-young. I am your cousin. I have two grasshoppers." She made a little hole at the top of the cardboard note and pushed the string through, then tied it tightly.

Na-young decided to send not only a letter to her cousin, but also something special. A special gift. What else could she tie to the string? The bag of candy kept high on the pantry shelf? Her favorite yellow dress? Maybe her colorful rock from beside the front door?

She chose the rock. It was gray on the outside, but purple on the inside. Her cousin would love it. Na-young carried the rock inside and tied it to the string just above the piece of cardboard. Then she opened the door. She pushed the balloon up into the air so the breeze would catch it.

The balloon did not fly. It dropped to the ground and skidded along slowly into a fence on the west side of the road.

She retrieved the balloon and brought it home. It was just too heavy to fly. She reduced the weight by untying the rock. She dragged a chair from the living room to the pantry. She climbed on the chair and up onto a higher shelf. Then she reached her hand way up to the very top shelf and brought the bag of candy down. She tied the bag to the string.

She waited until a gust of wind came and then let the balloon go again! This time it slowly rose just a bit higher! She was so excited that she ran after it. But it floated north up the street.

The wrong way!

It finally bumped into a billboard
and got tangled up. She freed the
balloon and brought it home.

"My balloon must float higher," she thought. Na-young reduced the weight even more by untying the bag of candy. Then she changed out of her favorite yellow dress and tied the dress to the string instead, along with the note.

This time when she released the string
the balloon rose much more quickly.

But then it floated east toward the stadium.
Toward the Arirang Festival!

Dancers, flags, music! The balloon soared above the performers, high above the stadium, up towards three military helicopters! The helicopters hovered over the stadium, pushing great downdrafts of air with their rotor blades.

Down, down the air pushed the red balloon. Down, down to the ground, right in the middle of the performers! Na-young ran through the astonished performers and grabbed the balloon.

"My balloon must float higher!" Na-young ran home as quickly as she could. She knew she had to remove as much weight as possible from the string. She untied the dress and the cardboard note. Being careful not to poke the balloon, she used a knife to trim off almost the entire piece of cardboard, leaving only the "N"–the first letter of her name–so her cousin would know who had sent the balloon.

She had one last gift to give. A grasshopper.

She went to her box, opened the lid, and carefully picked up her green grasshopper. She let it crawl onto the "N". She tied the "N" to the string again. Then she opened the door, stood in the street, and paused. Na-young took a deep breath. She looked at her clasped fist. The balloon tugged on the string as she held tight. Slowly she loosened her grip, opening her fingers like the petals of a flower, and released the balloon.

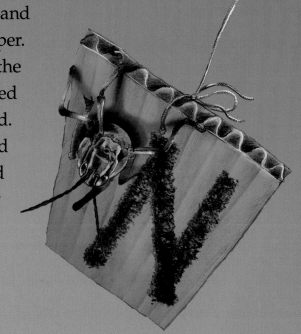

It zoomed skyward! A strong gust of wind pushed the balloon higher and higher, south toward the demilitarized zone. Higher still.

She leaped up and down with joy and then chased the balloon! It floated as high as the treetops. It floated as high as the birds. It floated as high as the clouds.

It floated towards the demilitarized zone and then sailed over the border as Na-young ran to try to keep it in sight. Over the heads of the North Korean soldiers! The soldiers saw it and pointed.

Then the soldiers noticed Na-young running towards them.
They frowned. They closed ranks and did not let her pass.

She peeked through their weapons.

Na-young saw her balloon fly over the heads of the soldiers from South Korea on the other side. Her red balloon looked tiny in the distance. A small "N" dangled from its string. She watched it gradually disappear far, far away.

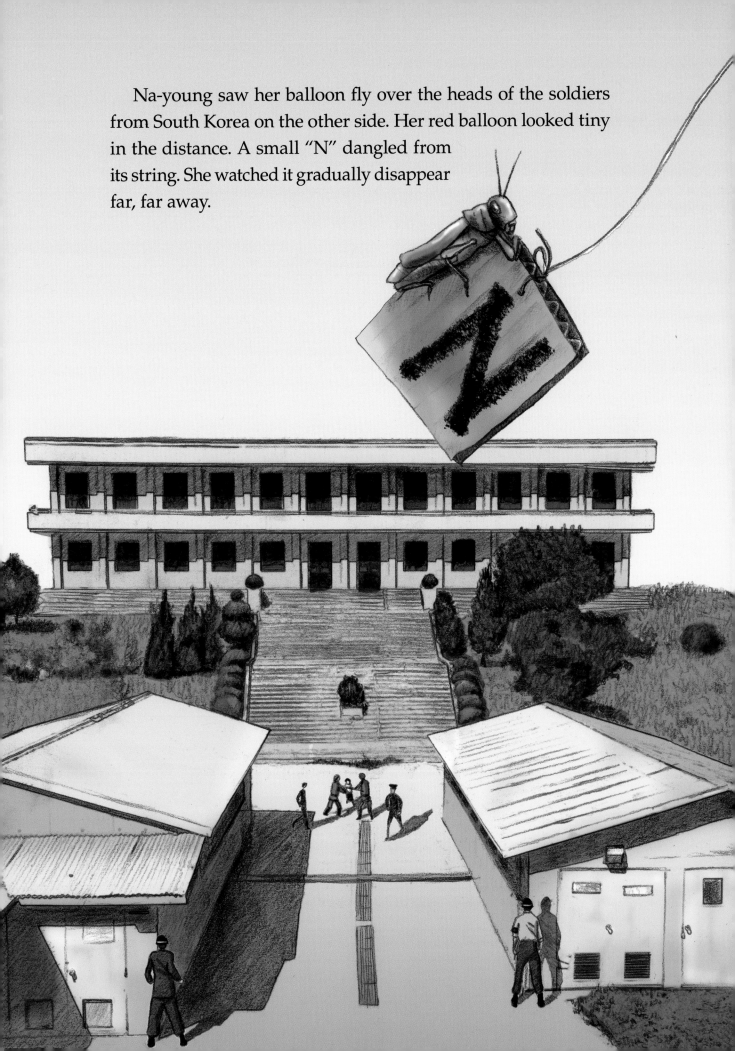

A child's work is to create the man he will become.
-Maria Montessori

A note to Parénts:

N is for North Korea highlights two of the fascinating educational principles found in Montessori schools. Notice how children can relate to *N is for North Korea* on a variety of levels. While one child might be captivated by the beauty of the balloon or by the girl's expressions, another child might be interested in the experimental process of flying the balloon. Yet another child might wonder about the curious billboards in the background, the Korean writing, the meaning of the guards and the guns, or the relationship between South Korea and North Korea. Likewise, the Montessori curriculum is individualized to meet the precise developmental level of each child within the three-year, mixed-age classroom. Each child progresses at his or her own pace.

Second, children in a Montessori classroom engage with the real world, both inside and outside the classroom, through meaningful, purposeful, self-chosen work. This emphasis starts with the hands-on practical life work that attracts very young children. It then leads to hands-on science projects, such as the one that so intrigued Na-young. By the time Montessori students are in middle and high school, they are venturing forth on almost daily "going-outs" in which they interact with adults out in their communities, apprentice with professionals, and run micro-businesses. Children in Montessori schools are given the opportunity, the respect, and the responsibility to grapple with real world issues. Even North Korea.

If you find these Montessori principles intriguing, you may be interested in visiting your local public or private Montessori school to see for yourself. Simply ask to observe a classroom.

An interesting piece of work, freely chosen, which has the virtue of inducing concentration rather than fatigue, adds to the child's energies and mental capacities, and leads him to self-mastery.
-Maria Montessori

FRIENDS FREE LIBRARY
GERMANTOWN FRIENDS LIBRARY
5418 Germantown Avenue
Philadelphia, PA 19144
215-951-2355

Each borrower is responsible for all items
checked out on his/her library card, for
fines on materials kept overtime, and
replacing any lost or damaged materials.